CLARY SAGE

CLARY SAGE

VICTORIA GODDARD

Oh, this one is for Lee (and also Lin)

Hal came fifteenth in his year's Entrance Examinations, which was not *bad*.

He was third-placed from Odlington, which was not surprising—Gidgeon was a major swot amongst even the swots of their school, and Jollimore was terrifyingly brilliant. Jollimore had come first in the overall list for Ronderell, and Gidgeon third.

And then there was Hal, fifteenth. His twin sister (his *younger* twin sister) had come eighth, which would please her. And their mother. Come to that, Hal was pleased for Elianne. They were both smart, but Elly had a gift for maths that he did not possess.

Even if everyone in the first fourteen places took up scholarships (and they didn't always, if the place they'd wanted had already been taken; Elly might or might not, depending if someone else had already chosen Quance before her turn), he'd still have most of the Golden List open to him.

Not to mention, it wasn't as if *Hal* needed the scholarship. So long as he passed, any of the universities in the Charter would most gladly take his money.

And his title.

Everyone wanted an imperial duke on their student roster. Hal had been receiving fawning offers since long before he was remotely of age to take them up.

He frowned at the parchment notice posted outside the Senior Common Room at Odlington. The main list was posted down in the town, outside the university hall where the Entrance Examinations were held, but Odlington School always got a second copy for themselves. Hal glanced in the open doorway, but the room was empty of professors and upper formers alike. Too hot, perhaps. He'd rather wished he could talk with Professor Bevan, his housemaster—insofar as Hal had *had* a housemaster; he hadn't ever lived in residence—but there wasn't much advice the man could give him on the subject of university that Hal hadn't already heard.

Not that it mattered, anyway. The Dukes of Fillering Pool always went to either Tara or Zabour, and since Zabour had fallen into the sea during the Fall, that meant Hal was going to Tara. Elly, as the younger twin, could go wherever she wanted— within reason, of course, but it wouldn't matter if she chose a lesser school because it had the best professors for her interest— not in the way it would for Hal.

Hal couldn't go to, say, Firbeth. Not even if it were reputed to have the best botanical gardens in Northwest Oriole. Firbeth wasn't even on the Golden List—it wasn't even on the *Silver* List. Nobody who wasn't interested in gardens had even *heard* of the university. Hal had only heard of it because he'd been poking around the stalls at the summer fair and found a book from before the Fall of the Empire describing 'Lesser Gems of Northwest Oriole', which had said its gardens were well worth the long detour to get to them.

He wasn't quite sure where Firbeth was, but that made it sound very well out of the way.

Regardless, he'd be going to Tara, what with Zabour having

fallen into the sea. Not to mention Firbeth was probably, oh, overrun with mandrakes or manticores or something.

Mandrakes would be better than manticores, obviously. Though weeding them might prove tricky—

He sighed and turned away, striding easily towards the school gates. The banner of Fillering Pool snapped overhead: the great black tree with the stars entwined in its roots. The Leaveringhams, the ducal family—Hal's family—were proud of their illustrious heritage.

Hal was proud of his illustrious heritage. He truly was. Each star represented a century his predecessors had been Imperial Dukes, entrusted by successive emperors of Astandalas with the rights and responsibilities of raising armies and feeding and outfitting them. Fillering Pool itself had generally provided officers (many of them going from Odlington to the naval colleges at Inveragory and Isternes) and ships; the men and food had come from other parts of the old demesne. Nine stars in the roots for nine centuries under Astandalas; and the tenth in the sky for the new direction to come after the cataclysmic collapse of that empire.

Hal dropped his gaze from the flag to the grounds. They were mostly empty, as classes were still in session for the younger years, but over by the gates were a cluster of young men lounging on the grass. Probably others from the upper sixth.

Now that the results were available, all Hal's fellow students would filter away to their universities of choice. He'd see a few of them again, no doubt. One or two at university, though Gidgeon was likely to go for Stoneybridge over Tara, they were reputed to have the better Faculty of Philosophy, and Jollimore had mentioned how he was wanted to go to the Bardic College of the University of the Outer Reaches when he'd come to Odlington.

A couple Hal might see at formal events, he supposed, but probably as—secretaries or stewards or similar. His years at

Odlington had been surprisingly light of members of the peerage.

Perhaps not surprisingly, given the Fall of Astandalas right around when he'd been supposed to begin attending. People who had survived had mostly kept their children at home. In other decades there might have been princes and viscounts and so on to keep him company, but as it stood ... Hal glanced around at the old stone buildings, warmly golden in the afternoon light, and then lifted his eyes up to the even older castle brooding above them. His personal banner—the tree black on a white field instead of white on blue—was no more than a bright spot from here. Showing he was in residence, as he always had been.

He'd been duke since he was seven. None of this was a surprise. It was just ... he supposed it was just that he'd put off thinking about what finishing Odlington would mean. That he would be moving on to the next step, the next stage, of life.

It wasn't strange he was perhaps a little blank at the prospect, was it? It was a big change.

At least he could put off thinking about marriage until after university. Even his mother was currently fretting over his cousins.

Most of his house—insofar as it was his house—were lounging on the lawn outside their dorm, enjoying the spring sun. They'd already have seen the results list, of course—it would have been posted early that morning. Hal didn't live in residence, since Odlington had been built where it was precisely so that the duke's sons could attend while still living in the castle. He stayed for most lunches, and occasional formal dinners, but the rest of time lived at the castle.

It would have been nice to live with the other boys, even if the meals were not anywhere near as good as he got at home. But when he'd been eleven and twelve there had been the strange, terrible period of the Interim after the Fall of Astandalas, when magic had gone entirely awry and the school had for the first time in its long history closed its doors. When it had reopened, and Hal had been able to go, he had been nearly fourteen, and there had been extra lessons he (and only he) needed to take, and meetings with his steward and bailiffs and chamberlain and groundskeeper and the mayor of Fillering Pool and all the other people who looked to the Imperial Duke as their liege.

Hal hadn't been able to come down for the ceremonial posting of the Exam Results because there'd been an urgent meeting with his steward, and all right, he was the duke, he was the only one who could sign the forms for releasing a prisoner— but did it have to happen on what was supposed to be one of the most important mornings of his life? It was supposed to be *special*, getting your results.

He sighed inwardly, not too obviously, smiling instead at the boys (young men, they were all young men now, seventeen or eighteen) before him. Gidgeon, Jollimore, Dwile, Shadblow, and Tuttle Major.

None of them were friends, not really. Hal could never participate in the after-hours fun and fights. The few times he'd tried there had been the definite sense he was an interloper, if not exactly unwelcome.

No one was stupid enough to be *rude* to the single greatest landowner and highest-ranked man left in Northwest Oriole after the Fall of the Empire, etc., whose family had been funding the *school* since its foundation. But they never let him forget any of that, either.

"Coming out with us tonight, Duke?" Dwile asked, because all right, Hal was a swot, too, in his own way, and he'd known them for years. And surely he wasn't wrong that there was a bit of fondness in them calling him 'Duke'? He'd wanted them to call him Leaveringham, but there'd been a bit of a fuss when someone who hadn't realized who he was mocked the pretentiousness of pronouncing it 'Lingham' and by the time the study hall proctor had finished *explaining*, there was no chance Hal was ever going to be considered one of them.

But then he wasn't, of course. None of them had inherited more land than the King of Rondé when they were seven. Even if half those holdings were now defunct, or at least lost, since they'd been on Ysthar, and Ysthar had been basically destroyed by the Fall. Even counting only the Alinorel holdings, Hal still owned more land than anyone else. Much good as that did him.

"Might be able to come by, if it's not too late. Where are you going?" he asked politely, nodding at the others. "Good show, Jollimore, Gidgeon."

He was *not* going to be embarrassed for coming in fifteenth. Elly could tease him all she wanted once she came home from her school (for, not being the duke, *she* got to board), and he would be glad for it, because she only called him *Your Grace* when she was mad at him.

They'd called the old duke, their father, *Your Grace*. Hal didn't mind from most people, but from family ... when he had children, he had sworn to Elly, they wouldn't call him that.

Jollimore looked smugly pleased; Gidgeon just looked smug. Hal supposed they'd earned it.

"Usual place, no?" Dwile said, blinking slowly at him, like a cat in the sun. Hal wished he'd realized how warm it was when he left the castle; the walk back up was going to be hot. They'd all taken off their dark robes and were lounging in shirts and trews, but Hal wasn't in the mood to start a rumour about his state of mind (on this day of all days, when the exam results were posted) by being anything less than properly dressed.

"We could go down now," Jollimore suggested. "Peardon's taken Zarouche to meet his parents."

Those were the last two in their house and form. Hal knew them even more peripherally; Zarouche had come in to take his room, he guessed, a year after the others. As for Peardon—well, as far as Hal had ever been able to tell, Peardon simply didn't like him.

There was a general murmur of agreement, a gathering of robes, and the group stood and reformed around him. Hal realized belatedly that they must have been waiting for him, and he felt his heart warm at the thought.

It was probably mostly Hal's fault they weren't friends, anyway. Elly had told him he was intimidating. Which must be true, what with the title and the castle and how he sometimes got called out of class to deal with his estate.

It wasn't that Hal *never* went out with the other students. And it wasn't as if anyone besides his mother or his aunt (or his sister, when the news eventually reached her) would chide him directly for anything he did—there were barely any *laws* that applied to him—but Hal knew that any slip of tongue or behaviour would be immediately pounced on. And then—

He remembered how when they were eight or nine, long before the Fall (but after the old duke's death), Elly had disappeared for most of a day, in which she'd made friends with a pig-farmer's daughter, been *given* a piglet, gotten into a fight (fisticuffs and all!) with one of the tenants who'd kicked a dog in her presence, and come home with both the pig and the dog, everyone had chuckled indulgently and let her keep the pets.

A few weeks later, Hal had visited the old herbwife at the edge of the forest, in sight of the castle no less, and they'd sent out search parties for him after barely two hours. There had been a whole article in the *New Salon* about it. And letters. And they'd called for the physician, in case he was ailing for something.

It just wasn't the same, that was all, for him and Elly. That was fair, wasn't it? Elly didn't get to be duke, because she wasn't the eldest, and Hal *did*. So it was only fair Elly got things, some freedoms and indulgences, things Hal didn't, in exchange.

The usual place was down in the town, near the market square. It was a student pub, cheap and unrefined; Hal had only been a handful of times. It was always different, when he came. At some point *someone* would realize he was there and even if no one came to ask him for anything, they still always went on their best behaviour, and that meant *he* had to be on his, and—and no one enjoyed going out for a drink and having their landlord and lord watching you, did they?

He bought the first round, naturally, and before he sat down with the others he told the barman to put all Jollimore's and Gidgeon's drinks on his tab, because they *had* done best in the exams, and Jollimore at least had no money—he was at Odlington on a scholarship—which Hal knew (though it was kept quiet from the other boys) because he had to sign off on the school's budget and grants each year.

That done, he snuggled into the back corner between Jollimore and the wall, where no one was likely to see him accidentally, and sipped at his own ale. It was good, on such a hot day. Everyone else had opened their robes again, or divested them entirely, and Hal was struck by a surge of jealousy that they could just *do* that.

But he could do things like pay for Jollimore's and Gidgeon's drinks, he reminded himself. He could leave that fifteenth place open for someone who didn't have his resources, so they could choose a university they might not otherwise be able to attend. He could support Elly against their conservative relatives in going for whatever degree she wanted. Hal would never have to worry about a roof over his head or how to keep himself busy and productive.

No one *was* looking at him. He moved discreetly and opened the neck of his robes. If he'd dared—

Jollimore was looking at him, eyes briefly narrowed before

he smiled. Hal smiled politely back and dropped his hand to cup loosely around his tankard. No, he didn't dare. The pub wasn't full, by any means, but there were other students celebrating their exam results at other tables. No one else from Odlington, but that just meant they were complete strangers to Hal. Most of them looked far too absorbed in themselves to care if the young nobleman in the corner loosened his robe, but they would care if they caught the duke using magic.

It took half a tankard for the group to relax into conversation, but fortunately the rest of them were much faster drinkers than Hal, so it wasn't too long before they were chatting about their plans.

Hal found himself strangely disinclined to announce he was going to Tara. He sipped at his ale, listening as Dwile and Tuttle Major teased Gidgeon about whether third place was going to be sufficient for, yes, Stoneybridge. "Jolly might claim your place, you know," Tuttle said slyly.

Jollimore shook his head but didn't say anything. He had messy dark hair and mid-tone skin, and striking ice-blue eyes. Hal never felt quite so obvious next to him, though his own skin tone was so dark a brown as to be nearly true-black; the other students ranged from Shaian brown to the older Oriolese pink and pale-buff tones.

"Are you going to the Outer Reaches?" Hal asked Jollimore curiously, when Gidgeon had turned to Dwile to interrogate him about how he'd definitely not be getting in to Oakhill on merits, not with a thirty-seventh placing in the results. Dwile seemed entirely unmoved by this argument, but then his father had remarried an heiress after Dwile's mother died in the Fall.

"What makes you say that?" Jollimore asked, narrowing his eyes again, his face suddenly hard and intent.

"I thought you wanted to go to the Bardic College," Hal replied, trying to remember if he'd ever heard Jollimore ever say otherwise. "If you've changed your mind, of course, that's your business. You certainly have the results for anywhere you please."

"We've never talked about that. Your Grace."

Hal felt something shrivel inside him at Jollimore's suspicious tone and that deliberate, painful courtesy. "I remembered you mentioning it, that's all," he said, the polite easy tone he'd been taught, glad for the tankard in his hand to provide him with something to look at. "I asked my mother about it. She said it was very highly regarded."

"You asked your *mother*?"

No one else was paying any attention to their quiet conversation in the corner. Shadblow was talking about the rival merits of Lambert and Harktree for medicine, which Tuttle Major naturally had opinions on, as his father was the royal physician in Kingsbury. Tuttle Major was going to go to Lambert for medicine, same as his father.

The door to the pub banged open, letting in a welcome gust of cooler air along with a less-welcome crowd of other students. Gidgeon got up and went over to the bar to get another pitcher of ale, and looked confused when the barman refused his coin.

Jollimore was staring at Hal with real surprise.

Magic was more than out of fashion, since the Fall, most places. Odlington *used* to teach it, as part of a well-rounded education, but the teacher had traditionally been a visiting professor from Zabour, and the last one had died with the Fall.

Hal had been taught at home. It was one of the reasons why he had so rarely been able to go out with the others. One of them. Elly had the barest gift and once she had the basics down, had not needed more than the odd holiday-time remedial lesson.

Hal was not powerful, but he could have been a good wizard, if things had been other than they were.

"She's always kept abreast on the various schools of magic," he explained, because the Bardic College was the pre-eminent school of musical magic in the world.

Jollimore turned in his seat so he could regard Hal directly. "And do you—or your mother—have any thoughts about it *now*?"

The Duke of Fillering Pool was *personally* responsible for the scholarship students at Odlington. Since Hal was so young, and a student there himself, his mother had gone to the teas and meetings in his stead since his father's death. But Hal had made sure he knew the current reputation of the places Jollimore in his year, and Dunbar in the year below, and Haigh below that, had in mind.

"They're fairly cagey, but my mother was a well-known practitioner, back before the Fall, and they were willing to tell her that they've kept their old skills up. It's safe to go there, if that's what you're asking."

"Why do you even care?" Jollimore asked. "I'm not ... like you."

Hal looked down at his tankard again. He still had a third of it left. He wanted to say, *Aren't you?* but he couldn't make himself say the words out loud. He knew what Jollimore meant.

The others were laughing, joking now about some girl Tuttle Major had his eye on.

"I'm not sure I can afford to get there," Jollimore muttered after a few moments. "Even with the scholarship covering tuition ... I've been saving for a fiddle, you see ..."

There was no actual request there. Hal had been the recipient of more than enough pleas to be able to hear that. For a moment—just a moment—Jollimore had forgotten who he was speaking to.

Hal wanted to sit there in that moment for as long as he could. But even before he started to reply, Jollimore looked up from his own tankard and flinched back. "I didn't mean—"

"No. I know," Hal said, not sighing, because he knew how

condescending his sighing came across to other people. But he wanted to sigh, he did, he told himself truculently. He wanted to sigh, he wanted to undo his robes, he wanted to be on his third tankard of ale, he wanted to be flirting with the girls at the next table over.

But Hal had been the Imperial Duke of Fillering Pool since he was seven, and filling the majority of his duties since his fourteenth year. At seventeen and a half he had a great deal of practice with restraining his sighs. And more happily, bestowing largesse.

"I am quite certain," he said, quiet and solid as the foundation stones of his castle on the hill, "that there is a sizeable prize for coming First in the Entrance Examinations. I expect it will be more than enough to get you to the Outer Reaches. And back," he added, for Jollimore did have family, didn't he? He went *somewhere* in the summers, at least.

Jollimore opened his mouth, no doubt to argue that there had never been such a prize before, before he looked down, flushing dully, and said, "Thank you."

Hal felt excruciatingly embarrassed, and turned away from Jollimore under the pretext of taking a mouthful of his ale. His motion caught the attention of Gidgeon across the table, who was just setting down the pitcher.

"Want s'more, Duke?" he said, not waiting for Hal to do anything more than set the tankard down. Hal watched him pour it warily, but the ale didn't slop more than a few drops onto the table.

"Go on, then, Gidgeon," Jollimore said, voice much lighter than it had been. And that was worth it, wasn't it? Hal was sure it was. "Have you situated everyone?"

"Everyone except you and his grace here. I'm for Stoney-bridge, you know, unless you take it. Or Elinor Bilbower, whoever she may be, curse her name."

That must have been whoever came second in the overall

list. Hal hadn't paid much attention, not knowing the name either.

"Wouldn't dream of it, you prat. I'm going to the Outer Reaches as soon as I can find a ship going north."

Jollimore's voice was cautiously excited, and Hal *was* glad. He made a mental note to check costs before he organized the prize. His steward could find out the cost of a berth to the Outer Reaches. Nothing too fancy—Jollimore would probably refuse that. He had his pride, and had earned it.

"And you, Duke?" Gidgeon said. The others all fell silent, turning towards him, even Tuttle Major leaving off his flirtation.

Of course they wanted to know. That was natural, wasn't it? It wasn't just ... Hal couldn't think what *use* it would be for them to know. It wasn't as if it would be exciting news for the *New Salon* or the Kingsbury papers or anything.

"Tara," he said indifferently. "The dukes have always gone to either Zabour or Tara." He shrugged, which his governesses would have deplored, but they were at the pub, and if he couldn't shrug here, then where, honestly.

(One of his governesses would have said, *Nowhere, your grace*, and rapped him over the knuckles with her pointer, but she hadn't lasted long; Elly hadn't responded very well to her instruction. Hal was very grateful to Elly. If only Odlington hadn't been a boys-only school—but for some reason that was enshrined in its charter, and Hal was seemingly the only one who'd ever wanted to change it.)

He became aware that Jollimore and Tuttle Major were staring at him. He raised his eyebrows in reproof, and Tuttle Major looked away.

Jollimore said, "Where would you go, if—if that didn't matter?"

Hal blinked at him, as slowly as Dwile, if hardly as cat-like and content. The others were all listening, even Shadblow, who had barely ever interacted with him.

Surely they knew that wasn't how it worked? Hal had always known it *did* matter.

And it wasn't as if he didn't *want* to fulfil all those expectations. He was proud of his history, of his family's history, of the long traditions he had inherited and would tend and pass on to those who came after him.

There was no way he was going to say *Firbeth*. There would be too many questions about where it was and why and—and that *would* be news, wouldn't it? There would be a froth of rumour and reports about his state of mind and his marks in the exam (no matter that he'd come *fifteenth*) and what disgrace he must be hiding, and—

Anyway, probably there were no great gardens left in Firbeth, after the devastation of the Fall. And it wasn't as if Hal actually *knew* if he really liked gardening. He was good at natural philosophy, and liked botany, and he enjoyed being outside and looking at plants. But then again, he wasn't nearly as good at sports or physical activities as Elly; he'd probably hate a practical course such as Firbeth's apprenticeship in the botanical gardens. Which they almost certainly didn't still offer, anyway.

He smiled, and sipped his ale, and lied through his teeth. "Never thought about anywhere else."

❧ 2 ❧

The others were drunk enough they did not let this go.

Hal honestly wasn't sure what to do when people just … didn't let it go.

He could make a fuss, he supposed, when Gidgeon and Tuttle Major started analyzing everything they'd ever noticed about Hal's scholarly interests. He could have said, coldly, in his best ducal tone, *I shall be going to Tara*, or *I don't see how it's any of your business*, or … or there were a lot of things he could say, in fact.

But Tuttle Major was talking about the speech Hal had given for their Rhetoric class last year, and of course it was a good speech, Hal had been instructed in how to give a good speech since he could *talk*, but—

But Tuttle Major remembered how Hal had argued for the validity of legal codes with all his examples being drawn from mixed-up common names of plants.

It wasn't that strange, Hal thought mulishly as Dwile and Tuttle Major snickered about some of the ruder names for bleeding heart. Plants were very interesting, and the history of their common names—clary, for instance—

Tuttle Major was going to Lambert to study medicine, like his father, he'd said proudly. (Why was *his* desire to follow his father's footsteps met with cheering, and Hal's—) Dwile would go to Oakhill, and Shadblow wanted to study naval engineering, of all things, at Isternes, and—

"Professor Bevan said he should go to Morrowlea," Jollimore said, and everyone fell silent to consider this.

Hal was letting it all wash over him. Their arguments were interesting, to be sure, he was—pleased—yes, pleased, that they'd apparently been paying so much attention to him (but then he *was* the duke, that was the fundamental thing *about* Hal, he was the Imperial Duke of Fillering Pool, people always paid attention)—

The corners of his jaw were tight and prickly with tension. Hal kept his face polite, even when they all fell silent and stared speculatively at him.

People had been staring speculatively at him his entire life. That was just the way it was. People looked to him.

"Morrowlea, hmm," Gidgeon said, affecting a ponderous tone and stroking an invisible beard. "Tell us more, Jolly."

But Jollimore smiled and said nothing, and after a few moments the others started to give their thoughts.

"It's one of the Three Sisters," Dwile began.

"Very true," Gidgeon acknowledged. "Entirely respectable for anyone. Simply *anyone*."

The Three Sisters—Tara, Stoneybridge, and Morrowlea—were the oldest and most prestigious universities in Northwest Oriole. Tara was the oldest and arguably the *most* prestigious—as well as the closest geographically to Fillering Pool—which was why the dukes had usually gone there, if not to Zabour.

Zabour had been *their* university, like Odlington close to home, and when it was the duke rather than the heir who was attending, they would invariably have gone to Zabour so they could keep fulfilling their duties even during term.

It would have been no question at all, if Zabour hadn't fallen into the sea. Hal had enough of a gift of magic he could have studied that—Zabour had had a very respectable Faculty of Magic in its day—and he would have been able to live in the castle, at home, at least half the time, and—

And Zabour *had* fallen into the sea, so it would be Tara. They didn't have anyone currently specializing in botany, and of course magic was entirely out, but Hal had already received a strongly suggested course of study that had been followed by 'many of your grace's distinguished forbears'. Tara's Triplum of economics, political philosophy, and law was rightly well-regarded and would no doubt serve him very well.

"Morrowlea's radical, though," Shadblow said doubtfully.

Of course it was Shadblow, who was almost incredibly conventional. Hal sometimes watched Shadblow's reactions to ideas or propositions just to get a sense of how the general populace was likely to respond. He'd very rarely been off the majority response. Hal had certainly found it wiser not to rock any boat Shadblow found unstable.

"Exactly," Tuttle Major said, and when Hal, despite himself, looked up at him, the other student smiled.

Morrowlea *was* radical: that was its reputation. Excellent scholarship, and a fermenting froth of egalitarian politics. They maintained (and yet their results remained at the same heights as the more specialized schools) that their students ought to be well-rounded and capable at all levels of society. There were rumours that no one was allowed to use any titles at all, at Morrowlea.

Hal should not, he was sure, have even begun drinking the second tankard of ale. He could feel it as a warmth in his cheeks (though that might have been the heat in the room, which remained sweltering), and though he was still in control, he was not quite so in control he didn't answer that implicit challenge.

"Why?" he said, tasting the bitter ale on his tongue. "So I can learn proper humility?"

Shadblow and Dwile both drew in their breath sharply. Tuttle Major glanced at Jollimore, and Jollimore at Gidgeon, and it was Gidgeon who said, "So you can s-study what you want for once."

Hal could not stop the laugh from bubbling up, though he was able to swallow it back soon enough with a mouthful of ale.

The old duke had studied the magical properties of wool; but then the wealth of Fillering Pool proper was in its sheep, and its woollen mills. And its shipyards, and its fisheries. A few mines. Magic, once upon a time. (Rents from its very wide-spread tenantry, always.) It was not, and never had been, in its verdure. (Hal had some ideas—he'd read a few things about soils and how to improve them—but—he could study that on his own time, of course.)

And the old duke had died when Hal was seven, and so his opinions, whatever they might have been, didn't matter, did they?

"I'll be taking the Triplum, I imagine," Hal said, knowing his voice was flat and tired, but he was suddenly exhausted at the thought of all the *gracing* and curtseying and—

And that was an intolerable affront to the people who looked to him, to his tenants and populace, to all the people for whom Fillering Pool was a more important title than the regional duchy of Ronderell or even the kingdom of Rondé. All those people who depended on him being the best duke he could be.

Jollimore said, "Tara doesn't even *teach* botany—"

"Then I shall study it in my spare time, which is what people do, isn't it?" Hal said, and this time he couldn't manage a smile. He set down his tankard. "I must be off. Good luck with things. Gentlemen." He stood and nodded at them, and walked off before they could say anything else.

He wished Elly was home. Though she'd probably agree with them, and that wouldn't be good, would it?

Hal and his mother (and the various second and third cousins and honorary aunts and uncles and miscellaneous friends of the family who lived in the castle) celebrated his results with a meal of all Hal's favourites, which he appreciated. His mother was clearly pleased he'd gone out with the other students, though she made a face at the smell of ale when he first came to greet her.

She didn't ask where he intended to go. He thought she might, at one point, but then he said he'd be writing to Tara soon, and she nodded in acknowledgement. Before she could ask about his program of study, he mentioned the idea of a prize for the person who came First in the year's Entrance Examinations. Discussing that took up the whole second half of supper, and he was glad.

Not that there was any reason he should be *glad* not to talk about his own prospects.

Not prospects. It was too set for that.

The next stage of his life, he supposed. He would spend the summer getting all his affairs in order so that his mother and various officers could take care of things—and then he would go to Tara to study the Triplum.

It would be interesting to live in residence, or at least in the vicinity, at least. The university had sent him some information about the various options, helpfully pointing out which they thought were the most appropriate for his rank and station. As the Leaveringhams had not maintained a residence in Orio City since the Fall, there was, he was informed, a row of townhouses that their more distinguished students often preferred to rent.

That would no doubt assist in meeting someone who would

be acceptable to his family for a bride. Once they graduated, of course.

It was all very straightforward. Hal had always appreciated how ... how set it was. It made it easier to focus on the things he *did* need to decide on, all the things his steward and bailiffs and chamberlain and men of affairs brought to his attention, if he knew that all he had to do was ... step onto the next flight of stairs.

He wished Jollimore hadn't put any ideas into his head. He kept wondering about Firbeth, wherever it was, and an apprenticeship that he would never be able to serve. As for Morrowlea—

It didn't really matter what *Hal* thought of Morrowlea and its radicalism. Shadblow's uncertainty certainly reflected what the general response to that choice would be, and Hal already knew he'd be fielding questions about Elly going to Quance for maths.

Besides, the Triplum would be useful. The university had sent him an outline of the courses of readings, lectures, and sample papers for the first year. It would be good to read over some of the texts again, he was sure. Surely he'd learn *something* new. Perhaps in the upper years. The professors couldn't expect that their students came in with ten years of training for and three years of active experience in a leadership role, could they? He hadn't read most of the books for classes at Odlington, after all, but for his summer tutors and extra lessons. The Taran professors quite reasonably expected none of their students would be taking up any positions until after their degrees.

Hal could imagine there would be nuggets of wisdom in the lectures, and perhaps he'd learn things in conversation with the other students. And there were a few texts in the first year's curriculum he hadn't read for years. It would be good to go over them again, no doubt.

And yet, when his great-uncle came to visit a full fortnight after the exam results were posted, Hal had somehow still not written to Tara to inform them he was taking up a place there.

Everyone *thought* he had. Hal had written the letter, even. It was in the drawer of his desk, in the pile of drafts that no one else looked at. Sometimes, when no one else was in the room, he pulled it out and read it over again, intending *this* time to seal it and place it in the tray for the footman to take to the post office.

And yet, each time, he found himself putting the letter back in the drawer. There was something about the phrasing that sounded off, he told himself. Eventually he would figure out what it was.

His great-uncle, Uncle Ben, was his favourite relative. Besides his sister and his mother, of course. But of all the rest, it was Uncle Ben by far. He was old, but still hale; he'd been an officer in the Astandalan army his whole career, and was a much-decorated general. He advised both his brother the King of Rondé (sometimes) and the Lady of Alinor (more frequently) on military matters, but when he was not with the lady on Nên Corovel he often stayed for weeks on end at the castle.

One of their traditions, started when Hal was quite small, was that as soon as Uncle Ben came, they would go for a walk.

This time Uncle Ben arrived mid-morning, having stopped for the night before at a friend's manor a bare few miles from Fillering Pool. Hal had already met with his steward and was going through the accounts. He was pleased to see that the new fund for the Annual Leaving Prize—for the highest result in Ronderell, not simply at Odlington school—was properly set up and that there would be a prize-giving ceremony the next week, presumably when Jollimore's family could come to see it.

"It's a beautiful day out," Uncle Ben said when he entered Hal's study. "Come for a walk?"

The words were ritual. No matter the weather, it was always a beautiful day. Hal smiled, left off his accounts, and moved to accompany the old man outside.

It was, surprisingly, a genuinely beautiful day. Hal hadn't been out that morning, and he was grateful to stretch and turn his face to the sun for a few minutes.

They didn't talk at first, or not to each other. Hal greeted the servants and other people they passed as they came through the castle and into its courtyard, and then they turned to go through the orchard and thence towards the pastures running down the back side of the hill, away from Odlington and Fillering Pool town.

One thing Hal had always liked about his great-uncle was that they *could* be quiet together. Hal loved his sister, he truly did, but she often made him feel as if he was staid and boring and much more than an hour and a half older than she.

Uncle Ben said it was too many years in the army that had roughened his edges, but other members of the family said he'd always been wild. But then he was a younger son, and by the time his brother had become King of Rondé there had already been others in the succession, so he was like Elly, and hadn't ever *had* to be ... tamed wasn't the right word. Constrained, maybe. Sometimes Hal felt very constrained.

Uncle Ben liked telling stories about his time in the army, which Hal usually liked, but he didn't think he could bear to hear of all those travels and great comrades at the moment. (Because even though a general and a prince, Uncle Ben had somehow managed.) And he couldn't—absolutely couldn't— find the words to say anything about his plans. Uncle Ben knew about them, anyway. Everyone knew Hal would be going to Tara.

Eventually he thought he should ask about the political situation in Nên Corovel, or failing that the one in Orio City, which was the largest city on the continent and former capital of the Imperial Province of Northwest Oriole before the Fall of the empire. And where Tara was located, of course, though Hal sometimes forgot that.

But though he opened his mouth to ask, the air was so lovely—cool up here on the shoulders of the crag, with the young apples showing through the leaves in the orchard trees, and the sun bright in a blue sky dotted with puffy white clouds, and it was so very much early summer in all her finest glory that Hal just didn't want to ruin it with that sort of topic.

He cast around for another subject, and quite involuntarily, because he'd once had the thought that Uncle Ben might know, he said, "Have you ever heard anything of Firbeth recently?"

"Firbeth? The place west of Harktree, you mean?"

Hal hadn't even been sure where it was. "Yes, I think so."

"They had a bad fire there a few years back, didn't they?" Uncle Ben hummed as he thought. "Yes, that's right. They had a famous arboretum—had trees from all over the Empire. Lost everything, I expect, when those wildfires swept through. What made you ask about them?"

"I hadn't remembered about the fires," Hal said quietly, grappling with a foolish, foolish sense of disappointment. It wasn't as if he'd *really* thought of going there. It was far too far away, if it were past Harktree, for one thing.

"Hal, is anything wrong?"

"Of course not," Hal said, turning his head away so Uncle Ben wouldn't see him blinking. It was just a bit of dust from the trees above them, catching in his eye. He put his hand on the gnarled trunk of the old apple tree nearest him, breathing in the kind scent of the green apples and growing things around them. The bark felt good under his hand, as if it were scratching an itch he hadn't known he had.

"Hal."

There weren't very many people who could say that to him, in that tone. Who *would* say that to him. His mother had less and less often as he'd gotten older. Partly this was because Hal didn't give her *reasons* to use it, and partly because Elly did. Sometimes that was as camouflage for Hal, which he could only appreciate. Elly understood him in a way probably no one else could.

She'd be home soon, at least. Her school was in Kingsbury, which wasn't far, but her term ended a week after his, and she'd lengthened the journey a bit by staying a few days with several different friends along the way. He couldn't begrudge her that —her friends would be scattering to their various futures, too, this year.

"Elly's very happy to be going to Quance," he told his great-uncle, and why had he said *that*? That was—Hal smiled determinedly, though he couldn't meet Uncle Ben's eyes. "She's already been corresponding with the professors of mathematics, seeing which of them will suit best."

"That's good," Uncle Ben murmured, and for just a moment he put his hand on Hal's shoulder. No doubt it slid off because Hal had just that moment started walking again.

"Yes," Hal said, and resolutely talked about Elly's plans until they had left the orchard and were walking across the grazing meadow towards the woods. The old herbwitch had died several years before, and her cottage was falling into the vegetation she'd once grown for her remedies. Only the wooden bench where she'd used to sit, sorting her herbs, was still solid.

Hal catalogued the plants he could see as they came closer. Feverfew, vervain, balm, costmary, foxglove, woolly mullein, woundwort—

"And what about your plans? You must be looking forward to Tara."

"Of course," he said, and could find no more words. Lungwort, sneezeweed, elecampane, horehound, mint. In the sunnier patch, half a dozen kinds of sage.

('All the salvias are to be respected,' the herbwitch had told him, letting him pluck leaves of each, from the woolly silver sage to the nubbly grey-green common cooking herb to the great soft chenille-crinkled clary sage. That was blooming now, great wands of large dusky pink flowers, which the herbwitch used to hang to dry. 'Plenty of uses,' she'd told him, shaking a bee out of the hooded flower it had rested in. 'Clear sight and soothing balm, and beauty too.')

After a much too long a pause, Hal said, "It will be ... most educational to spend time in Orio City." That hadn't come out too stiffly, had it? He licked his lips, trying to recall what he'd been telling himself for the past fortnight. "I'm sure the Triplum will be very ... useful."

Uncle Ben was silent for a long while, and then he said, "Oh, Hal."

He opened the sagging gate around the old cottage and sat down on the bench. "Come humour an old man and sit down with me."

As if he had to ask. Hal sat next to him, remembering those handful of stolen visits with the old herbwitch, how she'd taught him the plants in her garden, all their old country names. The scent of thyme and lavender was heavy on the air here, and the bees sounded drunk on nectar as they buzzed around the clary on either side of the bench. Hal took a deep breath, feeling his shoulders relax. It was easier to look at the castle on the ridge above them from here.

How he loved Fillering Pool, he thought absently. He didn't have much magic, really, but he could feel the land in his bones.

"You don't have to go to Tara if you don't want to, Hal."

The same bubble of laughter came up, though this time he didn't let it out as more than a smile. "Zabour's not an option," he murmured.

"Would you have gone to Zabour over Tara, if you could?"

If they were on the other side of the castle, they could have looked down over Fillering Pool to the harbour, and on the further side of the harbour might have seen the ghostly towers of Zabour catching the odd glint of light. The actual stones and earth had all long since disappeared under the water, but the spectre of the ancient university still hovered there. It was most visible under moonlight, but you could see it during the day if you knew what to look for.

"I would, yes." That was safe enough to say. Zabour had been acceptable.

"Why?"

"It's closer," he said. "Ruling dukes always went there, because they could—I could—be here for anything I'm needed for. And ... it would have been interesting to study magic, I like to think."

"More interesting than the Triplum."

This was not the pub, and Uncle Ben was a prince and a much-decorated general, so Hal did not shrug. He nodded once, slowly. Surely he didn't have to pretend to *like* it? It was going to be hard enough to listen to Elly's enthusiasm about Quance without that.

"Hal, you're named for me," he said.

"Yes." Uncle Ben's full name was General Prince Benneret Halioren, and Hal was Halioren Lord Leaveringham, Duke of Fillering Pool, etc. There'd been another Prince Benneret when Uncle Ben had been named, hence the unusual double fore-name. Hal had a middle name, Isidorus for his father, but that was unusual too.

"Would you do something for me?"

"Within reason, of course," Hal replied, smiling at his uncle, glad for the change of subject. "What would you like?"

Uncle Ben hesitated, and then he said, very seriously, "Go somewhere else. Pick something *you* want to do. You know more about politics and economics than most of those professors, and you'll hate Tara. It has no greenery and it's foggy all the time. Your mother is perfectly capable of managing the dukedom if you go further away."

Hal swallowed very dryly. "I'll still be the duke," he pointed out, and why had he said *that*?

But Uncle Ben started to smile. "Oh, is *that* the problem?" he said, putting his knobbly old hand on Hal's knee. "I had wondered, you know. Elly said it was probably—But that's easily dealt with. If you're serious."

"If I'm serious about what?" Hal asked, suspicious about the sudden undercurrent of glee in his uncle's bearing. "And what's this about Elly?"

"She's been worried about you," Uncle Ben said gently. "We all have. No one's heard you laugh since the exam results came out. Your mother is very concerned."

That did make Hal stiffen. "It has nothing to do with the results. It's nothing to be *concerned* about if—if I'm not very excited about Tara," he said. "I'm sure it'll be fine."

"No one has heard you laugh in *weeks*," Uncle Ben repeated, and Hal looked down, at the creeping thyme and tiny-leaved Corovel mint between the old bricks underneath the bench. The old herbwitch had told him how the Corovel mint was useless for anything medicinal and had a strange camphorous scent, but she'd loved the miniature leaves and how the prostrate stems hugged every crevice and bump in the bricks.

"I've been busy. Things piled up while I was studying for the exams."

"Here's a question," Uncle Ben said, ignoring this. "If you could go somewhere where no one knew you were the duke— where no one would *find out* you're the duke unless you told them—would that be something you'd like?"

Hal reached down and pulled off a sprig of lavender. "What a question."

"It's not a trick, Hal."

Hal had not bothered to look into any universities besides the ones the scholarship students were interested in and Quance, for Elly. He knew things about them, of course—one could hardly avoid learning—but not even his housemaster Professor Bevan, who'd gone to Galderon during the Scholars' Revolt and was something of a radical himself, had actually come out and said that Morrowlea was *that* extreme. It would have to be Morrowlea, if that sort of anonymity were a real possibility without actual falsehood, which Uncle Ben would know Hal couldn't countenance.

Uncle Ben waited while Hal systematically destroyed the lavender sprig. He leaned back against the bench, turned his face to the sun, and sat there smiling. It was all most irritating. Hal knew very well his uncle would not let it go until he made some form of an answer.

But if he said it out loud—if he agreed—what then? If he broke generations of practice and tradition in this matter, what was to say he wouldn't break generations of traditions and practice in others? He could not forget how Shadblow, always that barometer of general opinion, had looked so very doubtful at the mere mention of Hal going to Morrowlea.

Hal had never lied to his uncle, and he didn't intend to start now. He looked at the flecks of purple and green on his fingers. The lavender was pungent in the air. He breathed it in deeply. "I don't know if it's something I would *like*," he said, "because I've never experienced what it's like, not being the duke. Not since —since the old duke was alive."

The old duke. Never, not once, *my father.* But then Hal had some complicated feelings about the old duke, and his death, that he didn't like thinking about if he could avoid it.

He hesitated there, watching a bee crawling over the Corovel mint near his feet. The insect didn't seem bothered by the camphor; it was quite thoroughly absorbed in the small pale-purple flowers.

"I wouldn't mind," he added at last, uncomfortably honest, rubbing the nubbly lavender florets between his fingers. "I wouldn't mind, I think, having the chance to find out."

❧ 3 ☙

Unlike Tara (or indeed several of the colleges of Stoneybridge), Morrowlea had not bothered to send a fawning letter to the Duke of Fillering Pool. Its twin reputations for radicalism and scholarship had been maintained for several centuries, and although the nature and degree of radicalism obviously shifted over time, it was nevertheless true that it had always been that bit too radical (and that bit too far away) for the Leaveringhams. As far as Hal knew, not a single family member had gone in at least two hundred years.

Hal wrote to them, a formal letter of enquiry, barely daring to ask what their faculty of natural philosophy was like. He didn't tell anyone that he'd written. Not even Uncle Ben. Not even Elly. Though the only reason he got away with that was because she wasn't home yet.

Not that Morrowlea was going to refuse him entry. He had come fifteenth in the exam results, and even if Morrowlea only took about fifty students a year, half of whom were drawn from the top placements in each of the regional examination lists from the original Charter of Universities— Morrowlea had an extremely small incoming class—he was within that range, and of course he wasn't asking for a scholarship. Just a place.

The letter came nearly by return of post, which shouldn't have disappointed him. He was the Imperial Duke of Fillering Pool—of course they'd reply immediately. Of course.

He always read his correspondence in the duke's study, or rather it was his, of course, but he hadn't ever changed out the furniture so it was always, in his mind, *the duke's*, which ... well, that was probably a little sad, wasn't it? Elly always said he could at least replace the pictures with ones he liked, but Hal actually rather liked the landscapes. And the portrait of his grandfather's setters was by Doiron, and that was valuable.

He made himself read through his other letters first. Elly's was bubbly and cheerful, though now that he'd talked to Uncle Ben, he could see that she *was* a little worried about his mood. He scrawled a short note. *I'm fine, Elly*, he wrote. *Enjoy your visit with Lisalot. I'll see you when you get here. I'm not going anywhere.*

Finally he couldn't put it off any longer. He opened the envelope, fingers straying over the heavy wax seal of the university, and took a deep breath before unfolding the missive.

The letter was from the Chancellor herself, and was short and to the point.

Your Grace:

I received your letter of application with some surprise and, dare I say it, intrigue. While your results on the Entrance Examination are entirely satisfactory, and I have no doubt your scholarship will be at the level we expect, we seek students who will particularly thrive in the culture we have striven to nurture here at Morrowlea. You will be aware of our reputation for radicalism, and have nonetheless written, so it may be that you will be one of those students.

To be clear, we seek to foster both independence and interdependence. Our students come from all walks of life and all regions of Northwest Oriole; we do not believe that those accidents of birth we call rank have any bearing on potential or capacity. Thus we insist on a kind of anonymity for our students: those who come here are known not by their titles or trappings of wealth or poverty, but by their own merits. All titles (and necessarily surnames) are, in fact, concealed from all the students, staff, and faculty bar myself and my assistant, who deals with student correspondence.

In response to your other question, our Faculty of Natural Philosophy is very strong, particularly for Botany, Geology, and my own studies in Weather. Incoming students all take a set course of study for the first term to permit them to explore new fields of study and learn some of the practical tasks of living we expect our students to graduate entirely familiar with, so you need not decide on your direction immediately. We believe quite strongly that students should have the opportunity to try and fail at new things as well as succeed at what they already know.

Please note that students are not permitted valets, maids, or other attendants. The students are responsible for tasks such as cooking, cleaning, managing the stables, and producing the food and other materials required, as well as their studies. You need not be concerned if you are unaccustomed to any or all of these; we do anticipate the need for appropriate instruction. We take great pride in that Morrowlea is very nearly self-sufficient. All you need bring are two changes of ordinary clothes (such as would be worn by a prosperous country gentleman or, I might say, your grace's secretary or steward), toiletries, and personal belongings; whatever you bring, it should be no more than you personally can carry.

If this speaks to you, I would be most glad to welcome you on the twelfth day of September for matriculation. If you choose another path, I wish you all the best.

Rusticiana an Dirondelle, Chancellor of Morrowlea

. . .

Hal put the letter down with shaking hands. His first thought was to go talk to Uncle Ben, or to his housemaster at Odlington, or his mother, but … but he didn't dare ask them what they thought, did he? They all thought he would do splendidly anywhere he went, that he was capable of any challenge, that he was … He didn't even know how to finish that thought.

Elly wasn't here, but she would just say—

He tucked the letter into his pocket and went out, forgetting until he was halfway down the hill that he hadn't put on his coat. It was a hot day, and he hoped no one would think ill of him for that minor misstep. It wasn't as if he'd taken off his shirt, and he had a waistcoat on. It still wasn't at all the fashion to be in his shirtsleeves.

As he came near the Odlington gates he saw Jollimore coming up towards him. He was accompanied by an older couple: the man had Jollimore's pale eyes and raw build, though he was pale-skinned, and the woman Jollimore's messy hair and dark complexion. His parents, then.

The man was wearing a clergyman's collar, and the woman had properly upright carriage and an elegant tilt to her chin. Their clothes were not new, but well-made and mended. A rural priest and a poor cousin, Hal guessed, then remembered the letter in his pocket and felt uncertain of that sharp assessment.

But … he could make the assessment and leave it there, couldn't he? He'd already known Jollimore hadn't any money to speak of.

"Your grace," Jollimore said, stopping before him and bowing slightly, properly.

"Jollimore," Hal replied, equally politely, and felt the letter as if it were a brand in his pocket. He cleared his throat. "Your parents?"

Not that he wouldn't have greeted Jollimore anyway, not that he wouldn't have asked for an introduction—

Jollimore didn't seem at all surprised. "Yes. Your Grace, my father the Reverend Jollimore, and my mother, Mrs. Jollimore née Alberry. Mother, Father, this is his Grace, the Duke of Fillering Pool."

The elder Jollimores bowed and curtsied, and Hal nodded back, dipping into a slight bow for Mrs. Jollimore. Alberry was a good name; the more prominent members were at the court of the King of Rondé.

"Are you on your way to the school?" Hal asked politely, stepping back, though now that he'd seen Jollimore he wanted to ask him—tell him—he wasn't sure what. Tell him he'd written to Morrowlea, maybe. Ask him if ... if ...

"We're meeting Todd's teachers," the Reverend said, smiling fondly at his son. "We've come up from Elladale for the prize-giving ceremony. We're very proud of him."

"With good reason," Hal replied, which was the simple truth. "He's a great credit to you."

"We're very grateful for the scholarship that meant he could come to Odlington," Mrs. Jollimore said. Her accent was well-educated, her tone earnest but not pushy.

"I'm glad," Hal said. "It was established for that purpose, after all."

"And then for him to be able to go to the Outer Reaches— we understand we have you to thank for that, your grace."

Hal smiled uncomfortably. He wished he was dressed properly. "Not at all. It was all Jollimore's doing he came First in the Entrance Exams."

Mrs. Jollimore tilted her head and let it go. "And you, your grace? What are you plans for the coming year?"

He should have said Tara, of course. But the letter in his pocket felt as weighty as a stone. And Jollimore was looking at him, eyes narrowing more the longer Hal hesitated, and Hal didn't—couldn't—

"I'm still deciding," he said, as if it were easy. The elder Jollimores accepted that as being perfectly reasonable, but

Jollimore himself gave him a sharp, incredulous look. Hal looked back at him, knowing it would be rude to draw him away from his parents, and not at all wanting to talk about it in front of them.

But the Reverend Jollimore said, "Oh? What are you debating between?"

Which was a normal sort of thing to ask. If Hal had been a normal sort of person. He took a breath. If he said it out loud—there was no reason he could give to tell them not to tell anyone that wouldn't sound ridiculous. Hal could hardly say that he didn't want to start rumours in the *New Salon* or through Fillering Pool or anywhere that suggested he was unfit in any way.

"Tara," he said, which was utterly unexceptional, and then, trying not to sound reluctant, "and Morrowlea."

"Morrowlea!" the Reverend said, as surprised as Shadblow, and Hal braced himself because he'd known, hadn't he?

But Mrs. Jollimore was smiling eagerly. "Really? I went there, you know," she said, dropping most of her reserve and stepping forward. "Did Todd tell you? I was the Rondelan Scholar. I loved it. There's something so magical about the way they bring everyone together—a real community. If you're at all interested in—" She paused, obviously recollecting his position and coming to the same conclusion Hal had, that it was not *quite* the sort of place he should want to go. No matter its scholarly excellence. But then she said: "May I ask, your grace, what's making you hesitate? Do you have any questions I might be able to answer?"

It was because he'd forgotten his coat, probably, that she was being so informal. So familiar. Hal felt as if the rules were melting around him, as if the land was falling away under his feet, as if the very air were suddenly becoming impermeable.

That was a foolish image. The air was always impermeable. It wasn't the *air* that was wavering mist-like, like the ghost of Zabour catching the sun behind the walls of Odlington.

Did he have questions she might be able to answer? Mrs. Jollimore née Alberry, who'd been the Rondelan Scholar to Morrowlea. That was right, Morrowlea only took one student from the entire Kingdom of Rondé, rather than one from each of Rondé's component duchies as the rest of the universities did. Some historical oddity, no doubt.

Jollimore had never really talked much about his family. Not to Hal, anyway. Hal couldn't have come up with *Todd* as his first name, and didn't know what it was inevitably short for. But you couldn't be in classes with someone for three or four years without gleaning a few things.

He knew there was just Jollimore, and there was no money, and he respected and loved his parents very much.

(You could always tell. Tuttle Major got on with his parents as well; Dwile liked his stepmother and was afraid of his father; Shadblow was estranged from both of his; Gidgeon and his brothers were orphans of the Fall and raised by their aunt and uncle, who were strict but kind. And so on.)

He tried to make it into a joke. "I'm afraid I don't have very many practical skills," he said lightly. "I've been the duke since I was seven, you know."

"So I've heard," Mrs. Jollimore said, and regarded him for a long moment before turning to her son. "Todd, you've known his grace for years. What do you think?"

Jollimore met Hal's gaze squarely. He was smiling. (Why was he smiling? Because Hal had listened to him?—it had been Uncle Ben, really—though if Jollimore hadn't brought it up, Hal probably wouldn't have been so perturbed about the idea of going to Tara that all his family were *concerned* about him.)

"I think you'll do well, your grace," he said very simply. "I'm sure it will be a bit *odd* at first, but I have no doubt you'll become accustomed in short order."

Hal's hands were damp, sweaty. The heat, no doubt. Jollimore shouldn't have phrased it like that, as if the decision were made.

"It's odd for everyone," Mrs. Jollimore said comfortingly. "And everyone starts from the beginning with *something*. I hadn't a clue when it came to gardening, for instance, for all I'd been spinning and sewing since I was a girl."

"Was there much gardening?" Hal asked, because he couldn't *not* ask, not when the opening was there.

Mrs. Jollimore laughed fondly. "So much. The university grows almost all its own food, you know, and the students work the fields and gardens as part of their work rotations. I still grow most of ours."

"And flowers enough for church and chapel and every room in our house," her husband said, smiling at her.

"I see," Hal said, and looked away at a glint in the air. But it was just a gull turning and catching the light, not the ghostly towers of Zabour. He breathed in through his nose.

Jollimore caught his eye and nodded once, solemnly, seriously, as if to say, *you can do it*.

Could he? Or—Hal was sure he *could*. (Was he?) *Should* he, now—

The reverend said, "It looks as if someone's coming." He gestured through the school gates towards the professor coming towards them.

"I shall leave you to your tour," Hal said with alacrity. "It was good to meet you, Reverend, Mrs. Jollimore. I'll see you at the prize-giving."

They performed the correct curtsies, but before he'd done more than step back, Mrs. Jollimore said, "If Morrowlea appeals to you at all, your grace, it'll be well worth attending."

"And of course, you could always go to Tara next year if it doesn't work out," the reverend pointed out, just as the professor—their housemaster, Professor Bevan—joined them.

Professor Bevan greeted them all and obviously wanted to ask what this was all about, but Hal did not want to say it (not when the professor had apparently told Jollimore, told the others, that Hal should go to Morrowlea—for what if he *didn't*?), and because he was the duke no one was going to press. Hal felt a bit craven, not answering the implicit question. He took his leave regardless, confused and trying not to show it, and turned back to the castle.

Once he was away from the gate he paused to look over the chancellor's letter again. Not that he didn't have it half-memorized by this point.

One line jumped out at him on this read: *We believe quite strongly that students should have the opportunity to try and fail at new things as well as succeed at what they already know.*

Hal turned that thought over in his mind as he walked on up the hill. He knew he would succeed at Tara. It would be like Odlington, probably. He would get the new experience of living away from home ... but his valet would come with him, and there would be someone cleaning his space and mending the fire and all the rest of whatever people did to keep a household running. He'd go to his clubs—Uncle Ben had already inducted him into several in Kingsford, and the Orio City ones would be next—and he would mix with the right sort, and find some proper young lady of the appropriate rank to be his duchess after they'd graduated, and he could follow the steps ahead of him without any need to try anything new.

And he'd just be, always, the duke. Utterly unexceptional except in the ways that he was supposed to be. He could have a hobby for plants, as his father had had for wool, and no one would think it in the least peculiar. Or rather, it would be peculiar, but in the sort of way people thought acceptably eccentric.

It wasn't as if he wanted to go raising armies or anything. Which he could, if he wanted to. Legally, that was. The imperial dukes had started off as warlords dependent on and answering to the emperor alone, with the duty of raising the legions of soldiers that served the empire. The imperial dukedoms sprawled across the borders and boundaries of the old kingdoms and principalities, off-setting their cultural and political power. Hal—or rather, the Imperial Duke of Fillering Pool—still had that vestigial position, despite the magical collapse of the empire when he was ten. Eleven? That whole period was hard to remember. He just remembered the storms, and how Zabour had seemed to fall endlessly into the sea, and how his mother had fought to keep the castle's magic safe for those who had taken shelter within its walls.

Who *was* he, if he took away the duke? Jollimore seemed to think he was someone.

Come to that, Hal thought he was someone.

It wasn't that he didn't *like* being the duke; he just was. There was nothing to do about it, since Elly had said she'd murder him if he abdicated in her favour, and ... and it wasn't as if he weren't *trained* for it. For all his youth and inexperience, he wasn't doing too badly. He thought. His mother and other advisors would certainly not have handed over as many duties to him if they thought he wasn't able to fulfill them.

Even if his mother had been reluctant (he remembered that now) at first, but she had been so very busy attempting to do *something* about the broken magic in and around Fillering Pool she hadn't, then, been able to act as duchess-regent as well. And almost everyone else who could have been was sick or injured or entirely overwhelmed, and the people had wanted a symbol, and Hal, for all his youth, could be that. And he'd *wanted* to, had known it was his obligation and his role, and so what if he was coming to it younger than usual? Nothing about the Fall of Astandalas had been *usual*. And he'd managed. He had.

Then again—and it *was* an important consideration, wasn't it?—then again, he would probably be a better duke if he knew who he was outside of that.

And Morrowlea had gardens. Fields. And he would be expected—no, *required*—to work in them.

He looked around the close-cropped grass in front of the castle, imagining what might grow in Morrowlea, which was in South Erlingale. Or West Erlingale. The country had changed named any number of times, and people still used both; some thought the Rondelan duchy of Erlingale should reunite with their long-separated sibling and form a new country. Which—well—regardless, both Erlingales were hundreds of miles south of Fillering Pool. Inland, too.

He imagined what he might learn, and be able to bring home. Some of his land had once been much more productive of wheat and vegetables than they were now—the old folks remembered when his grandfather had brought sheep down on what had once been fields.

He could learn that, at Morrowlea, maybe. Not estate management, which he already knew, and had excellent stewards and so on to keep teaching him, but how soil worked, why plants grew, *how* to grow them better. Things they didn't know. The farmers had a lot of knowledge and wisdom, but they had been hit hard by the Fall, too, and a lot had been lost in the storms and destruction of the Interim. Losing Zabour's library and archives had been a fell blow.

And—he paused at the crest of the hill to look at the glinting, ghostly towers, and then at the town spilling from castle to harbour, with Odlington tucked halfway down. He could see Jollimore and his parents crossing from the dorm to the eating hall, no doubt seeing all the sights.

Imagine making friends who did not know he was the duke.

He shied away from that thought. But yet—Elly was going to be at Quance, and she had plenty of friends. She was always on him to talk to more people. It was just that Hal was so busy, and he had so little in common with anyone except perhaps Jollimore, and that hadn't ever gone anywhere, obviously.

Though if he were at Morrowlea there was no reason they couldn't write to each other. Hal would be quite interested in hearing about the Bardic College of the Outer Reaches.

If it appeals at all, go.

Hal hesitated one more moment, and then he picked up his pace, the letter in his hand, aiming for his study and his seal. If he hurried he could make the next post.

$\maltese$ 4 $\maltese$

Hal decided to send the letter of acceptance and a promissory note for the first term's tuition before he told anyone, and then after he did so, still didn't tell anyone. Uncle Ben seemed to feel he'd given enough advice, for though they went for several walks alone together, he didn't bring it up again. Instead Hal got to hear all about Uncle Ben's friend and subordinate officer, the great hero Mad Jack Greenwing, who had saved his life more than once.

It didn't matter, anyway. Regardless of where Hal was going, he was going to be away from Fillering Pool for extended periods of time—months at a time—and so there was a great deal to prepare. Not to mention he was out of school and thus had more responsibilities, and so he was closeted in with the steward and accountants and secretary and his own piles of record-books and correspondence for most of every day.

So it was easy, really, not to tell anyone. It wasn't just that he didn't know how to explain what he'd decided, that he'd decided, that ... that he hadn't done what he'd said he would do. What everyone expected him to do. What everyone had been telling him he was going to do for as long as he could remember.

It was foolish altogether, he knew. His mother and Uncle Ben had *said* they wanted him to do what he wanted—Elly had been after him for *years* to loosen up—and they'd left him alone to make the decision, hadn't they? They weren't going to think *less* of him for having decided to go to Morrowlea after all.

He thought. He hoped. (He kept worrying about Shadblow's doubt, that surprise in the Reverend Jollimore's face, the fact that Morrowlea had *never* come up as a potential option except right at the end, when Hal had already resigned himself to Tara.)

Elly wrote to ask if he minded if she spent another few days with her friend, who was apparently having a rough time of it for some reason, and she sounded so diffident and torn Hal knew his own letters must have been sounding whinging and sad.

And so—

It was right his twin sister was the first one he told. Bar Jollimore, of course, but that had been more accident than anything. And he hadn't *told* Jollimore he was definitely going. Just that he was considering it.

Which meant he was. Hal didn't waver over decisions very often. He did his research, prepared what was necessary, made the decision, and moved on. There were so many things he had to decide on, as duke, things that *mattered*, were sometimes life-or-death to people, that he'd learned early not to vacillate.

I've changed my mind, he wrote to Elly, after half a dozen false starts. *I've been accepted for a place at Morrowlea. They have a much better natural philosophy faculty than Tara, I've heard.*

He wanted to say the other things, but if Elly had a fault it was that she sometimes read letters aloud in company, if she didn't think they were private. Most of the time that didn't matter, but he didn't want her to be reading an innocuous comment without realizing he'd started telling her secrets.

If they were secrets. But Hal didn't know how to say that he wanted to see what he was, who he was, when he wasn't the duke. Not in a way that didn't sound as if he were deprecating his rank and prestige and privilege. It wasn't as if he was trying to get out of being duke. Not that he could, short of destroying everything generations of his family had worked to build, or—well, he guessed he could move upwards. Elly sometimes joked that there was a vacancy for an emperor, now that Astandalas was gone.

Hal sometimes had nightmares about being forced to reconquer Northwest Oriole.

That was a better thing about Morrowlea, too, he reflected. He had to keep circling the idea, reminding himself why it was all right to choose that, pile up all the reasons why it was a good decision. There wouldn't be the sycophants and toad-eaters at Morrowlea; they wouldn't be pouring dangerous ideas into his head.

Or at least, not ideas that ended up with him raising an army and annexing the rest of Northwest Oriole into his holdings. Quite the opposite, probably.

Telling Elly helped lighten his heart, make it real. He found he was sleeping better, and certainly found it easier to smile. (And laugh; though he was sure he'd been laughing before, no matter what Uncle Ben said. Elly's response, which was in full, *Thank the Lady!* had made him laugh so hard he'd teared up.) Certainly his mother and Uncle Ben and the rest of the household were all quietly glad he was happier, even if they didn't know why.

For he still hadn't told them. Not yet.

And then they were having supper one evening, and after a break in the conversation his mother said, "Hal, darling, who do you think you'll take with you?"

"I beg your pardon?" Hal set down his knife and fork. His

mother was known for occasionally dropping entirely unrelated comments into conversations—she had a very active mind, and sometimes forgot no one else knew what she was thinking—but that had even less relevance than usual. Or maybe he was just preoccupied wondering about the flora of Morrowlea. He'd been looking at the atlas in the duke's study, and discovered there was a great vale near the university where an ancient inland sea had once been.

"This fall, when you go to university," she clarified. "I've been wondering if we'll need to take on any new staff. If you're planning a full travelling household, for instance."

Hal looked down at his plate. His face was burning. He should have told them a week ago.

"I was presuming you didn't want to stay in the common dormitories, but of course, if you'd prefer—"

"I'm not going," he blurted.

The room plunged into silence. His mother, Uncle Ben, the second and third cousins and the friends of the family and the upper steward and the chamberlain and all the rest: all of them stared at him.

"Not—not at all?" his mother said at last. Her voice was steady, and her eyes concerned, but Hal saw her hand had tightened on the stem of her goblet.

For someone in his position, to decide not to go to university at all—

That would be a scandal, and a big one. They would wonder at his health, his capacity, his schooling, his ... everything. Even if it wasn't exactly *necessary* to go to university to learn how to be a duke. He'd been doing all right all this time, hadn't he?

But he wanted to be more than *the duke who inherited when he was seven*.

"Not Tara," he said, and he took a deep breath at the relief in her eyes, and he saw the bracing smile Uncle Ben was offering him, and he lifted his chin and he said, "I'm going to Morrowlea."

"Oh," his mother said, and then again, more quietly, "oh."

Of course they were surprised by Morrowlea, but everyone would be. *He* was surprised, still, every time he looked at the letter he'd received back from the Chancellor after he'd sent the tuition.

You had a harder decision than most, she'd written. *I am confident you will like who you find yourself to be here.*

The summer disappeared even more quickly than usual. Hal felt as if, once he'd told everyone, he turned around one day to discover it was September, and time to ... go.

Quance was in Chare, not far from Stoneybridge, so he and Elly were going together as far as the border city of Givrène, where she would head southeast to her university and he would go southwest to his.

Southwest on the *stagecoach*.

They did not start off with the stagecoach; far from it. They were starting off with the ducal carriage.

"There you are," Elly said, when she found him standing at the window overlooking the courtyard where the carriages were being readied. "Is that really all you're taking with you?"

Hal had a small trunk with some finer clothes and books for the road, which would be returning with the carriage to Fillering Pool, a leather book bag Elly had bought for him, and an old army rucksack Uncle Ben had scavenged up from somewhere containing his *required belongings*. Hal was really not sure that seven pairs of breechcloths was going to be anywhere near enough. But then presumably there would be launderers.

Or laundry, anyway. Would they be doing that, too? He

doubted it; but then again, the Chancellor *had* said the students were responsible for everything.

Hal had never actually even seen the castle's laundry facilities. Sometimes he saw the sheets hanging out to dry in the sunny back courtyard. So that happened.

Down in the courtyard, the servants were wrestling with Elly's three trunks and a whole pile of miscellaneous other baskets and bags.

"This is it," Hal agreed. He had his two changes of ordinary clothes in the rucksack, a new set of toiletries (also from Elly, who had taken great glee in pointing out to him that his usual set of combs and razors had the ducal crest engraved on them), several blank notebooks, several books, and his favourite pen nibs and holder.

Every time Hal looked at the rucksack he felt a surge of disbelief that he was really doing this.

His valet, who had been the old duke's before him, was coming on this last journey—unspoken but clear was the idea that Hawking intended to ensure his grace did not embarrass anyone before he went off to join the great experiment of Morrowlea—and then taking the opportunity to retire. Hal had been trying to persuade the old man to take his pension for several years, so was glad for it.

Elly was bringing her lady's maid, an undermaid, and then there were the footmen and the coachman and a stable-boy, plus two outriders, and Hawking. They were, therefore, taking two carriages—one for Elly and Hal (and two footmen on the back), a second one for Elly's luggage and the rest of the staff.

It was not an unfamiliar production; any journey Hal had ever made had been similar. But he found himself watching it with new eyes, now that he was about to step aside from the great current that had been sweeping him along the path so many of his forebears had taken.

He'd managed to persuade the *New Salon* to say nothing

more than a coy 'prestigious institution' as his destination, knowing his appearance and accent would spoil the game if people at Morrowlea knew to expect him.

Somehow, the papers seemed to have had just as much fun gushing about Elly's new fashion of hat. Hal felt a little miffed that they'd let it go that easily, after all. Not that he wanted them to be making more of a fuss than a handful of articles speculating on which prestigious institution he'd chosen. Morrowlea was mentioned as one of the Three Sisters, and then immediately dropped; the writer appeared to believe that he must have chosen a lesser school if he didn't want to announce it to everyone. Hal was—relieved. And miffed. But at least they'd landed on 'wanted to do a heart's degree' as opposed to 'unfit for his role' as the interpretation.

"Your last week as duke," Elly said, leaning against him so she could look down on the courtyard.

"I'll still be the duke at Morrowlea," he murmured, leaning back. "They just won't know it."

"I think you're going to surprise yourself."

"Only myself?" he asked, trying to sound teasing rather than uncertain.

She poked him in his side, making him splutter and smile, and she grinned at him, satisfied. "Everyone, but mostly you. You'll impress me. Though you'll have to try hard to do that."

"I'll do my best," he said, laughing, and tucked her arm into his so they could go down to where their mother was waiting to see them off.

They were physically quite similar, Hal and his sister. They shared their mother's long nose and near-black skin, the old duke's fine features and zigzag coils of hair, their maternal grandfather's warm brown eyes ("just the colour of the dog's,"

Elly had once proclaimed). Elly was a bit shorter and a bit slenderer, Hal broader in the shoulder, but since Elly loved all things sporty and Hal did not, that was not so strong a distinction as it might have been.

But where Hal was careful, cautious, considerate—deliberate (he said)—forced to be staid (said his sister)—Elly was all merry and blithe and energetic and good. Born under a fortunate star, people said, and then, when they recalled that she was the duke's twin sister, hastily pointed to his wealth and standing as comparable evidence.

More to the point, Elly was entirely without qualms at the idea of heading off to university, and it was only years of training that kept Hal from being a nervous wreck. He had only looked back on the castle once after they left, when they turned from the approach onto the main road south. They were winching down his banner. Because he was no longer in residence. It made him feel shivery. It was mostly anticipation. He was fairly certain it was mostly anticipation.

Elly let him stew for the first day or so of their journey. She filled him in on all the news of her wide circle of friends, whom she'd spent much of the summer visiting. She had a handful of responsibilities as his sister and heir—if something untoward happened to him before he had children she'd inherit, and so needed to have a solid grounding in the basics of his role—and of course she had her own fortune and properties to look after, in preparation for when she came of age.

One of the trade-offs, again. Hal had the greater rank, fortune, responsibilities; Elly had much more freedom.

They'd spent a fair amount of time together, even with his duties and her travels—riding together every morning she was home, paying a few calls in the vicinity of Fillering Pool together, and she'd cajoled him into attending various teas and picnics with her friends—but not so much she didn't still have plenty to tell him as they journeyed south.

Hal had much less of interest to say. Since he hadn't read anything new, and Elly had gone with him to the few plays and musical performances he'd attended that summer, and she was not particularly interested in the affairs of the dukedom, there was ... nothing much else there.

Perhaps when he had some ideas for restoring the lost fields, restoring the heart of the land, he'd have more to tell her.

(Whatever else Morrowlea did for him, it would be full of new activities, new ideas, new things—things he could write to Elly and his mother and Uncle Ben, things he could tell them when he was home on holiday, things that *he*, Hal, could explore and see if he liked without wondering what everyone else would think. Or how much they were modifying whatever-it-was for his delicate ducal sensibilities.)

So Elly talked, and Hal listened, and sometimes they read their books, or Elly did and Hal tried to, and Hal quietly and discreetly fretted.

On the second day, Elly put her ribbon firmly in her book to mark her place, took his book out of his hands, set them both down, and said, "Hal. Stop worrying. It's going to be fine."

He looked out the window at the uplands of Lind. "That's easy for you to say." She scoffed and, nettled, he went on. "*You* don't have any reason to worry."

"Neither do you, Hal."

All the things he was worrying about seemed to rise up around him in a great cloud of dust and smoke. He took a deep breath, forcing them down. It was true his mother and his steward and bailiffs and men of business and so on were all very capable—more than capable—of looking after things for a couple of months. They had taught him all he knew about the matter in the first place!

Elly shifted over so she was sitting closer to him on the bench. "What do you have to worry about that I don't, then?"

She knew about all the ducal responsibilities. "You've been

away for school before." He flicked his hand at the window, at the view that could have been near Fillering Pool—all sheep and upland pastures—and sank into the velvet seat. "You know how to talk to people," he muttered. "People like you."

"They'd like you too, if you let them. They will like you."

His turn to scoff. "If I'm not intimidating with my title, then I'm boring. Neither is very reassuring."

"When have I ever said you're boring?"

"Countless times."

She dimpled at him, which was entirely unfair. "I've said you're *being* boring, which isn't the same."

"A nitpick."

"A nice distinction."

But he found himself smiling, just a little.

"Hal, you're my twin—and I'm not in the least boring. Ergo you can't be either."

"Your syllogism is faulty."

"My silliness is unflawed."

Hal laughed, and Elly smirked in satisfaction.

"You see," she said. "I'm not friends with boring people."

"I'm your brother."

"I like you," she assured him, dimpling again, then turned briefly more serious. "Hal, I know why you're worried, and it's not unreasonable. It's a new thing you're doing. I'm truly very proud of you. I'm so glad you decided to go to Morrowlea. And so secretly, too."

Hal twitched away, no longer laughing. "I had to," he muttered, which was something else their governesses had deplored. ("Always speak clearly and calmly, as befits the greatest lord in the land.") "What if I'd—not gotten in."

"Lady give me patience," Elly murmured, but she took his hand. "Hal, people do see the title first, and not you, I can't pretend otherwise. But that doesn't mean there's no 'you' under there. You'll always be the duke, yes, but you'll always be Hal, too. And Hal is an interesting, funny, friendly, intelligent, and *good* person. I can't *wait* for you to make his proper acquaintance."

Hal ducked his head and smiled reluctantly. But he did feel better.

At Givrène, on the border of Chare and Erlingale, they stayed in a fine inn worthy of a duke's sister. Hal had one last night under the ministrations of his valet, who took the opportunity of removing his boots to tell him a story about how the old duke had once gone out drinking with his friends in Orio City and ended up spending the night in a gaol. Which was perhaps intended to be a helpful story. It was hard to tell, what with the nerves currently churning Hal's stomach.

He was up very early. Hal had seen any number of dawns, and he was surprised it was still quite dark when he woke. They were further south, he supposed—Fillering Pool was almost at the northernmost tip of mainland Northwest Oriole—and the days were drawing in towards the autumn equinox. After washing up and dressing, he checked his rucksack and book bag for the tenth or fifteenth time, ensuring nothing in it was marked with the ducal crest.

He'd said good-bye to Elly the night before—she was not much of a morning person, being accustomed to the aristocratic round of evening engagements—and the stagecoach left early. He'd told Hawking not to worry about getting up either, in the interest of obfuscating his destination a little.

And so dressed in good but plain clothes—clothes such as he'd seen Dwile and Gidgeon and the others wear—which felt a little coarse and not quite fitting to his frame—Hal swung his bag onto his back and descended the stairs to the main room. He felt quite proud of himself for ordering a sausage roll and a cup of coffee for himself, and remembering to pay, too. From time to time he felt the stagecoach ticket in the pocket of his book bag. Hawking had bought that, or arranged it. But presumably by the time Hal was going home for Winterturn, he'd have found out how to get a ticket from Morrowlea.

He had just finished his coffee when the stagecoach came. Was it early? Perhaps not, as other passengers materialized out of shadowy recesses in the inn courtyard. The grooms changed the horses, and a few passengers disembarked, and Hal made his way to the coachman with his ticket.

"Up or in?" the coachman grumbled at him.

Hal was fairly sure Hawking would have bought the inside seat, but it was a crisp, clear morning, and Morrowlea was only a couple of hours away. And the thought of being squished inside with strangers—"Up," he said decisively.

"Good enough," the coachman said, and pointed to a very unstable-looking arrangement of protuberances Hal decided was probably supposed to be the footholds to climb to the roof. He made his way up with some difficulty, then settled next to a stout woman who was already seated there.

"Good day to you," the woman said, and Hal nodded back nervously as he tried to find a good place for his rucksack. He eventually stuck it between his legs, which was—very unducal. But then that was the point.

"Good day, ma'am." He was proud his voice didn't waver, even with trying to soften his accent a little.

"Northerner, are you?" the woman asked, shifting to make herself comfortable. "Hold on, lad, we're about to go."

Hal obediently held on to the railing around the top of the carriage, clenching his feet around his rucksack as the carriage lurched and jolted its way out of the inn courtyard and into the gloomy streets of Givrène. That was unfair. It was a misty predawn; he had seen Givrène was a perfectly pretty small city when they'd arrived yesterday afternoon.

"Yes, I'm from Fillering Pool." He realized belatedly he should have said *Ronderell*, because Fillering Pool might be too specific—might make people think of the imperial dukedom, and then, looking at his dark skin and features and hearing his accent, think therefore of the imperial duke—but the woman was clucking her tongue in consternation.

"Fillering Pool, Fillering Pool ..." She shook her head. "Surely I've heard of it, but can't think why. Is it near Markfen?"

Markfen was the capital of Lind, a good two hundred and fifty miles—and a country—south of Fillering Pool. Hal nearly drew himself up indignantly before realizing this was all to the good.

"No, ma'am," he said, smiling at her, relief washing over him. "Further north than that, past Ronderell, almost all the way to the top of Northwest Oriole."

"I didn't think there was anything north of Ronderell," the woman declared plainly. "You must be heading off to Morrowlea, with those pretty manners?"

Hal laughed, and swayed and lurched with the coach as the horses started to trot as they came onto the main highway, and he said, "Yes indeed! My first year. Are you from around here, ma'am? Can you tell me about the area?"

Because it turned out it was just fine to treat people like Hal had always treated people, if perhaps with a little more warmth and a little less stiffness, and certainly a whole lot less care about the proprieties. Or at least the Lady had sent him an easy person to begin with, for Madame Clegan, as the woman was called, was from Givrène and going to visit her sister in Déroue to the south of Morrowlea, and was happy to while away the journey after such an opening as that. All Hal had to do was watch his bag and his seat, and listen. And he could do that.

The stagecoach was much worse-sprung than Hal's coach, but it held together over the bumps and potholes of the road to Morrowlea, and Madame Clegan's continuous narration meant the journey passed quickly. Almost too quickly— Hal hadn't even had the time to work himself up into a great pother when the coachman drew to a halt outside a small country inn called the Morrowlea Arms and it was time for Hal to disembark.

He did so a trifle shakily, almost (but not) entirely from nerves rather than the jolting, and in short order found himself standing in the dust to the side of the road with his rucksack, watching as the stagecoach changed horses and an interior passenger struggled out. Hal dropped his rucksack, indignant that no one was assisting the lady, and was rewarded by a rather shy smile.

"Thank you," she said, in a southern accent—southern Chare, possibly? It was rather thrilling to guess, and to guess that he was not supposed to ask, not here at the very edge of Morrowlea—and she took a deep breath before smiling at him again, even more shyly but with a hint of excitement shining through.

Hal smiled back, feeling much the same. She was very plump, dark-skinned (if not so dark as he), and wore her hair in complicated braids.

"Are you a student as well?" she asked very softly.

"Yes," he agreed, and remembered his manners. Then he remembered halfway through what was an excessively ducal nod that he was supposed to be here as plain Hal, not a duke at all, and tried to turn it into a bow. It did not come off well, by her sudden cough and hand raised to her mouth. "This is my first year," he said, by way of explanation, and she laughed outright.

"Mine, too. I'm a trifle overset with nerves."

Nothing about her was much like Elly, except that Hal knew how to behave around those few young women who did not look at Elly's brother and see the most eligible bachelor in Northwest Oriole—he had long been exceedingly grateful that Elly had several such friends—and he relaxed, smiling at this new acquaintance as if she were one such sister's friend.

"Could be the springs on that coach," he murmured, delighted when she laughed again. He stepped back so he could pick up his rucksack. She had a small valise; just as much as *she* could carry. "I'm—" He only hesitated a moment. "I'm Hal."

"Hope," said his first fellow student, and smiled up at him. "Would you like to walk up together?"

"What a lovely name," Hal said, meaning it. "I'd love to."

Morrowlea crowned a hill in the rolling lands of West (or South) Erlingale. It was built of a pale limestone, and gleamed whitely in the sun as Hal and Hope walked slowly up the road past the country pub. One of the grooms had told them it was three miles or so to the gates proper, and they did not rush.

It was still quite early, hardly nine in the morning, and the air was cool and limpid, the light golden. Hope had a fair walking pace, and Hal matched it easily, as easily as if it were Elly he walked beside. They talked of a few innocuous things, the wayside plants whose names they knew, the beauty of the day, the glorious university awaiting them.

"It's hard to believe I'm really here," Hope said at one point, as they stood at the crest of a low rise and looked across at the towers and banners snapping ahead of them.

"I know exactly what you mean," said Hal. His own heart was beating rather fast. Not from the exertion, certainly. But excitement, anticipation, a small tremor of dread ... and curling through it all, like the first waves of a changing tide, the sense that all was in flux about him.

All *had* changed, surely. Hope was talking to him, a little shyly, entirely politely, her manners a little stiff but wholly proper—but talking. To him. Without a curtsey or a grace or the slightest hint she thought Hal intimidating in the least.

It was not surprising that he found that very odd.

Hal swallowed as they stood for a moment on the threshold of the great gilded gates, which were thrown wide in welcome, both he and Hope caught by the strangeness of everything before them.

Not that the university buildings, the handful of students in their robes, the professors in theirs, were *strange*. Except for all the ways in which that common and ordinary sight was coloured by the knowledge that in this place it was only their minds and their characters that mattered, not their wealth or rank or title.

Hal fiddled with the strap of his rucksack. Hope murmured something he couldn't catch; it sounded like a prayer. No one paid the least bit of attention to them, except for one older student hastening by on her own errands, who gave them a sympathetic, amused smile and said, "You'll be great. Go on over there, straight ahead. The Porter will tell you where to go."

And so they did: to the porter's lodge, where the Porter—another upper-year student—gave them a welcoming smile. "New students!" she said happily. "Welcome to Morrowlea! You're nice and early—must have come on the first stagecoach, eh?"

"Yes," Hal said, because nerves or no nerves he had been taught to speak when he ought. He reached into his bag for his letter of admission.

The Porter put up her hand hastily. "No, don't give me your letters of admittance—I don't need to know your full names! Show them to the Chancellor. She's waiting for you through there."

They passed through the lodge into the great quadrangle of the university. Four great buildings of splendid beauty faced each other across a lawn studded with huge trees, the five great oaks on Morrowlea's banner.

"They were planted by the university's founders, over a thousand years ago," Hal said to Hope. "Except that one—" He pointed to the central oak, still a magisterial tree but clearly centuries younger than the other four. "The original was older than the university, and was struck by lightning."

Or so he'd read in a book about the natural history of Morrowlea that Uncle Ben had found for him. It was a slim volume that had raised more questions than it provided answers. Which Hal had found quite delightful, since he was going to be able to see and research for himself.

"The limestone comes from the quarries south of here," she said to him, her eyes sparkling as she took in the sight. They walked down the gravelled central path to the smallest of the buildings, where the heavy iron-bound door stood propped open.

Another upper-year student greeted them and directed

them down the hall to another door, outside of which several chairs were set for those waiting. The door was open, and as they neared Hal exchanged a glance with his chance-met companion. "Would you like to go first?" he asked her, rejoicing in the ability to ask her, for all the precedents of the years had placed him first in almost every instance.

Hope flushed darkly, and she swallowed nervously, but squared her shoulders, lifted her chin, and nodded firmly. "Much obliged, Hal. Thank you for walking up with me."

"It was my pleasure," he replied, and this time his bow was much easier.

She giggled quietly and curtsied back, and then she knocked softly at the door and a woman's voice, cool as spring water and with the familiar court accent of Astandalas, bid her enter and shut the door behind her.

Hal sat down on one of the waiting chairs and did not even bring out his book to pretend he would read. He simply sat there, going over that hour's walk with Hope, burnishing the memory of his first interaction with a fellow Morrowlea student. If that was what it was going to be like ...!

It was perhaps fifteen minutes later when the door opened and Hope exited. "Go in," she said, fair glowing with excitement. "I'll wait for you, and we can walk over to the Sartor and so on together?"

Hal nodded, speechless at this easy companionship, unable to recall anything but that horrendous incident in study hall, his first day at Odlington, when Peardon had mocked Leaveringham and by the end of it everyone knew him for the duke. But he had been well trained, and he was grateful for that training as he set himself to his usual habit of posture and deportment and stepped through the door. He shut it carefully behind him. No footmen or maids here!

(And *what* a thought that was. Privacy, and ... labour. But privacy. Real solitude. It was—terrifying. But Hal didn't have to say that to anyone. Not even Elly.)

"Good morning, and welcome," the Chancellor said, regarding him with interest.

The Chancellor of Morrowlea was ranked equal to an Imperial Count; Hal bowed accordingly, rejoicing at the thought that this was the last time he would do so until he went home again. "Chancellor," he replied, straightening, and offered her his letter of admission.

Her eyebrows had risen slightly, and her face was amused. "I believe I know who you are," she said, taking the letter and glancing cursorily down at it. "I recall your father from my time at court. Indeed, your grace, you are *most* welcome."

"I believe it's Hal, here," he said with a small smile, and the Chancellor's answering smile was genuine.

"I am always glad to receive any of my students," she said, gesturing him to the seat before her desk. "Each of you come from such different backgrounds, and all have chosen Morrowlea for both scholarship and the ideals we stand for. I am particularly glad when we get the chance to welcome those who come from the more extreme backgrounds. Those who have lifted themselves out of poverty or isolation by their brilliance ... and those who have chosen to set aside all the privileges and powers they might command in order to learn a different way of being."

"I am grateful for the opportunity," Hal said, not pretending he was anything other than what he was—who he was. Who he was *now*, he the duke, with all the weight of his titles suddenly lifted from his shoulders. He would find out what that meant, besides an hour's easy conversation with a stranger. He finally had every opportunity and encouragement *to* find out.

He nodded at the Chancellor. "Due to my position, even with the measures I have put into place I expect a fair amount of correspondence. May I ask how that is organized? If I understood your letter correctly, only you and your assistant know our full names and standings."

"Yes, precisely. Sayo Swithin handles student correspondence; his offices are open at regular hours to collect mail or hand over items to be posted."

"And how is payment organized?" Hal asked, which was something he had never had to arrange for himself before and was quite proud of himself for remembering.

The Chancellor smiled at him with an ironic but not insincere eye. "Never let it be said that Morrowlea does not appreciate those of her students who pay the full tuition and thus cover the costs of certain things—such as the post—for everyone. Now, let us speak of other necessary matters ..."

He and Hope walked around the quadrangle following the directions of various upper-year students, first collecting their student robes and then seeking out their new residences. There were more new students arriving now, trickling by ones and twos through the gates and looking around with eyes as wide and awed and nervous as Hal had felt.

He felt much better for seeing everyone else obviously equally as uncertain at the newness, the oddity, the entirely strange situation in which they found themselves. With the bottle-green robes on over his plain clothes, he felt—different. Just Hal, for the first time in his life. None of the banners snapping in the light breeze overhead showed any of the familiar devices of Fillering Pool, and yet here he was.

"And here we are," Hope said, as they came to two buildings facing each other across a well-tended series of gardens. Vegetables, Hal thought, catching sight of what looked to be beans climbing up poles, but there were flowers too, full of bees and other insects, and there were birds too, and little wooden birdhouses for them on poles. He wanted—

He would have all the time in the world to look at those gardens. Learn the names of all the plants he did not know, how they grew best. His hands would feel the soil, and no one would tell him it was ignoble of him to desire to understand the ways of the humblest vegetables. He brushed his hand gently over the top of a long wand of clary, shaking the seedpods out across the path. For some reason there was one spray of flowers on this plant, months after the rest had finished. He wondered why that was—

He turned his attention hastily to Hope, who was smiling at him. "I can see something you're interested in already," she said gleefully.

He flushed, but he did not have to pretend, not here. "Yes. I like plants."

"I like stones," she offered back, just as quietly, almost as if it were as secret a yearning as his curiosity for the gardens and the mysterious ways of the plants that grew in them. Then she shook herself briskly. "I'm going to go find my room. And my roommate."

The Chancellor had told them they would be sharing, as a way of getting to know another student well (and to share chores and instruction with, at least until they began to know their skills and preferences after they had worked through the rotation). That might have put Hal off entirely, had he known before. He had been looking forward to having his own room in which to be himself.

But this was himself, wasn't it? A roommate wasn't going to change that.

He bid farewell to Hope, with a bit of a pang after her quiet, sturdy company, her quiet giggles, her shy but straightforward glances, and made his way to the second entry-door to the building, which was where his paper of instructions had told him to go. This was his bay, and his room was on the second floor—he climbed the winding stair past hexagonal landings set each with five doors, and a window on the outside wall—and found the door numbered 22c.

22c. Second door, second floor, third room of the landing.

Gingerly, he turned the handle, and let out a great breath to see the room was as yet empty.

It turned out they had their own bedchambers, tiny little closets as they were, but there were windows, and they would share a larger sitting room with a good fireplace and bookcases and old, homely furniture. Hal looked at the bare space, which was empty of art and books alike, but there were two desks, and two sitting chairs, and another window overlooking the gardens, and a tiny water closet to one side (albeit without a bath; those were shared with other students on the landing—the fifth door would lead there), and something in him unclenched.

He could handle this. A little bit of privacy, and yet company too. If only he got along with his roommate—

After some dithering Hal chose the bedchamber that had a view to a splendid copper beech, and he unpacked his few belongings into the wardrobe there, and then came out into the sitting room with his notebook and the intention of starting a little diary of his day.

And there was he was. His new roommate.

Hal looked at him, and his roommate looked back. He was pale-skinned but quite tanned, with dark brown hair that seemed a bit windswept or else as if he'd run his hands through it. He was dressed in clothes very like Hal's own, with his new Morrowlea robe draped over his arm. Short, lean, almost slender, and with narrow, handsome features Hal might almost have called elfin, except then he smiled and it was lopsided and nervous and sweet and steadied Hal's own thundering nerves.

"Hullo!" the newcomer said, half-bowing and then he caught himself, straightened, caught his foot on his robe, and tumbled over to sit on the floor staring up at him. He looked incredibly embarrassed. "I'm Jemis Gr—Jemis, that is. Jemis. At your service?" His voice trailed off uncertainly. "Or at least," he added, with another startling smile, "at your feet."

Hal laughed almost too hard with his nerves (but he had indeed been well trained and he knew to rein in his emotions before they became too hard to govern), and then, because he could—(he *could*)—he bowed courteously and then dropped right down to sit on the floor in front of Jemis. "I'm Hal," he said, smiling broadly at his own vast daring.

"I'd say I'm not always like this," Jemis said, "but that would be almost entirely untrue."

Hal laughed again, because—because this was what he had wanted all along, wasn't it? And oh, he liked Jemis already. And it didn't matter that he had a rural Fiellanese burr of an accent, or that Hal had no idea of his rank, or, or *anything*. None of that mattered. Just who they were in themselves.

"Don't worry," he said, "my sister tells me I am not actually boring, but I expect I'm close enough to balance you out."

His new roommate—new friend?—surely—surely—regarded him with thoughtful brown eyes. "Hmm," Jemis said, apparently wholly earnest, and then he laughed merrily. "First impressions say otherwise, but I'll let you know."

AUTHOR'S NOTE

This story takes place a few years before the beginning of Greenwing & Dart, in which Hal's roommate Jemis has a few adventures. (Don't worry, Hal is not entirely absent!) *Stargazy Pie* is the one to start with there.

For more about these and my other books, please see my website: www.victoriagoddard.ca.

www.ingramcontent.com/pod-product-compliance
Lightning Source LLC
Chambersburg PA
CBHW021744190726
48288CB00009B/3155